D1315301

For Matthew, of course
With special thanks to my writer
friends who help me along my writing
journey. - D. R. F.

For Connor, the boy who saved me
from an oncoming Dodge. - P. C. M.

Beep! Beep! Special Delivery
Copyright © 2019 by Della Ross Ferreri
Artwork Copyright © 2019 by Peter C. McEachen

Summary: Buckle up for an imaginative journey as one little boy has a special delivery to make – but he's stuck in a traffic jam! Beep! Beep! Ride along as he takes a short cut through the zoo, splashes down a jungle river – watch out for that alligator! – and climbs a steep mountain to make his special delivery.

Clear Fork Publishing
P.O. Box 870 102 S. Swenson Stamford, Texas 79553 (325)773-5550 www.clearforkpublishing.com

Printed and Bound in the United States of America.

ISBN - 978-1-946101-96-9

Clear Fork Publishing

BEEP! BEEP!

Special Delivery

Written by Della Ross Ferreri

Art by Peter C. McEachen

Beep! Beep! Hurry! Clear the way!

I have a special job today.

Traffic jam. Oh, what bad luck.

Can't get through with my big truck.

Look! A shortcut through the zoo.

Who hops by? A kangaroo.

Monkeys, tigers, ducks and swans,

Animals - come cheer me on!

Broken bridge! Look out below!

My truck can do it. Here I go . . .

Ka-splish, ker-splash, my truck can float.

Down the river, like a boat.

Jungle vines and hissing snakes,

Alligator! Hit the brakes!

Splash and swerve through swampy muck,

Gloppy mud. My truck is stuck!

Speed up – quick! – and plow right through!

Glub glub, vroom vroom, on my way.

My job is special. Can't delay.

Climb the mountain, to the top.

Don't look down.

A
mighty
drop.

Whoosh through clouds, my truck can fly.

Like an airplane in the sky.

Soaring, gliding through the air.

Getting closer . . . almost there.

Perfect landing. Made it through.

A special delivery . . .

just for you.

Della Ross Ferreri began the journey of writing for publication when her own children were young. Inspired by countless trips to the library and piles of picture books, Della joined SCBWI, took a writing class through ICL, attended conferences, and joined a fun and supportive critique group. Fast forward to today where Della is the author of picture books, board books and beginning readers. Her stories and poems have appeared in children's magazines such as Highlights High Five, Highlights Hello, Ladybug, Babybug, Boy's Quest, Children's Playmate and Clubhouse, Jr. She is a co-founder of Children's Writers of the Hudson Valley (CWHV), a volunteer group that organizes hands-on writer's conferences.

Della is a French teacher and lives in the beautiful Hudson Valley in New York with her husband, three children and two guinea pigs. In addition to writing and teaching, she loves spending time with her family and cheering them on at basketball and baseball games, and running races. Della also likes to cook, travel, read (mainly children's books), take leisurely walks and study French language and literature.

For more information about Della, her books and her author programs, visit her website: www.dellarossferreri.com

Pete McEachen is an Industrial Designer and Author/Illustrator living near Cleveland, Ohio. A graduate from the Cleveland Institute of Art, Pete found his passion in designing toys and cartooning. He began as an intern at Playskool, took a full time job at Little Tikes and rose to the position of Design Director. In 2010, Pete started his own studio primarily designing toys for clients all around the world. He was briefly syndicated with Universal Uclick for a comic strip called Mulligan and was also sponsored for a strip called Plugged In about a boy who wears hearing aids. Pete frequently illustrates as a diversion from toy design. He is adjunct faculty at both Case Western Reserve University and Cleveland Institute of Art teaching visual communication. Pete loves creating furniture for his home, talking cars with his son and discussing history with his daughter. He can be frequently seen shooing his cat, Horatio, off his drawing table or taking his dog, Cooper Edison, for a walk in the neighborhood with his wife.